Volcanoes

Holly Hoopoe's House

The Path to
the Big River

Poach and Coddle
Degg's Camp

One-Fang
Flossie

Riverbank

anana, Mangosteen,
and Durian Groves

Allie Croc and Friend

The Big River

Do Animals Cry?

Do animals CRY like me, like you?
　　Do animals cry—they do!
They may not shed tears like me, like you
　　But animals cry, they do!

When they've lost their home and they've nowhere to roam
　　When their rivers aren't clean and their forests aren't green
Then animals cry!

Yes, animals cry, they don't shed tears.
　　They have other ways to show their fears
Yes, animals CRY!

The Misadventures of Ori Tang

Original Illustrations by Alex Walton

Book design by Lee Edward Födi

Manufactured in China

First Edition

For information, please contact:

Brown Books Publishing Group

16200 North Dallas Parkway, Suite 170

Dallas, Texas 75248

972-381-0009

A New Era In Publishing™

ISBN13: 978-1-933285-85-6

ISBN10: 1-933285-85-0

LCCN: 2007928905

0 1 2 3 4 5 6 7 8 9

The Misadventures of ORI TANG

Written by **Sandra E. Stern**

Illustrated by **Alex Walton**

BROWN BOOKS · DALLAS, TEXAS

My name is Ori Tang

the
baby orangutan

(although I'm not a baby anymore, you know)

This story is all about ME and my family. We are your endangered animal friends. You will meet:

**Teena Tang,
my mother**

**King Tang,
my father**

**Uncle Cinnamon,
my big, fat, strong uncle**

**Kirstin,
my big sister**

**My many
cousins**

**Holly
Hoopoe**

**Figgy
the Frog**

**Poach & Coddles Degg,
the bad guys**

**Allie Croc
the Crocodile**

**Brenda
Butterfly**

. . . and many creatures of the rain forest where I live!

including One-Fang Flossie
the mysterious tiger

For all my children and their children
With happy memories of
My Father's smile
My Tony's spirit
My Hannah's guidance
My Bolivar's love.

Deep in the tropical rain forests of Indonesia live tribes of apes called "orangutans." Hidden in the heavy underbrush, these timid and shy animals keep to themselves. They spend their days swinging on vines, sleeping in trees, and socializing with each other.

King Tang, the giant ape, was the leader of a band of orangutans, and Teena Tang was his mate. King Tang and Teena were the proud parents of two orangutan children. Kirstin Tang was six years old and her baby brother, Ori Tang, was almost four. Compared to King Tang and his big, fat, younger brother, Uncle Cinnamon, Teena was smaller with soft, burnt orange fur and large, soulful eyes. She didn't have double chins like the adult male orangutans. She spent most of her time caring for her children and their many cousins.

Ori's daddy, King Tang, was the head of the Swinging Vine Academy where all the children went to school. The king made certain that everyone in his family became an expert in the ways of vine travel. They were taught to use their strength and agility. As a result, the Tangs always won prizes at the King Tang Vine Marathons. Being powerful, nimble, and swinging on the forest vines as a means of escape were the orangutans' only defenses against their enemies.

All the orangutan cousins tried to swing as high as the sky—higher than each other— but they would often slip and fall into the shallow pond below, where they ended up wrestling and play fighting. It was all in good fun, and Uncle Cinnamon kept a stern watch on them to see that they weren't too rough with each other. Keeping the young orangutans together was not an easy task. They were playful and curious, and they tended to wander off into the dense jungle.

The older orangutans were known to be solitary and shy, but the younger ones liked to talk to the birds, chase the butterflies, and play with the frogs. Brenda Butterfly and Figgy the Frog were Ori Tang's good friends.

The adult apes often argued. They chattered, they pondered, and they scratched. They liked to munch on nuts, berries, and insects, too. Although they were gentle and good-natured, they often complained about the noisy and really smelly hoopoe birds, the lazy crocodiles, and the risk of being caught by tigers (although there were very few around anymore).

There was, however, One-Fang Flossie!

The notorious tiger, One-Fang Flossie, lurked somewhere in the forest and often spied on the animals. Once, King Tang had seen her skulking around the pond and noticed that she had lost all her teeth except for one fang. The king reported his findings to the other orangutans, but that did not lessen their fear of her. Even the strongest ape, Uncle Cinnamon, was afraid of her. He had seen her tail a few times, but he always ran away before she could spot him.

In truth, One-Fang Flossie had become a vegetarian. She had lost all but one large tooth in an accident, and with only one fang, she could no longer charge and attack the animals.

Whenever she hung around the forest, all the animals could sense her presence. There was no chattering, squawking, or hissing. The animals maintained a strange silence, quaking and shaking in fear. They were afraid to move for they were sure she was creeping about, looking for something or someone to pounce upon.

The orangutans still believed that One-Fang Flossie was dangerous, and they cautioned their children to stay close to their camp and practice their vine travel. One-Fang Flossie still had a healthy and frightening roar.

Ori Tang was one of the youngest orangutan children. He was becoming very good at swinging on the vines, and his parents, King Tang and Teena, were extremely proud of their son. Ori Tang was filled with energy and was oh so curious about all the creatures in the forest. Although he was almost four and enrolled in the Swinging Vine Academy, he would sometimes forget to go to school. He wanted to explore.

Some of the younger orangutans were jealous of all the attention he got and were a little tired of his constant bragging.

Teena and King Tang laughed at Ori's mischievous ways, but they also fretted about him. Many orangutan babies were known to disappear, never to return, and it was difficult to watch the orangutan children all the time. Ori Tang was lovable and friendly, but quite a braggart, and extremely stubborn. How he loved to wander off and look for mangosteens—delicious, juicy red fruit.

Teena Tang loved to pick flowers for all the orangutan children, and she wore pretty flowers in her hair. Ori Tang wore a vine on his head to look like his father, the great King Tang.

eena often cautioned her youngest child not to wander off. There were many dangers in the forest, such as tigers and snakes and stinging insects. Ori always laughed and said, **"I'm not a baby anymore, you know."** He boasted that he wasn't afraid of anything or anyone.

There were many other dangers in the forest besides One-Fang Flossie. The rain forest was changing and the orangutan population was dwindling due to forest timbering. There were also fires and human poachers who stole baby animals. The orangutans became sadder and sadder as their rain forest became smaller.

Sometimes the older apes spotted two-legged creatures that seemed friendly and looked a little bit like them. They were men. They didn't have much hair, of course, but they were nice and often gave the orangutans fruits and nuts to eat. However, all the Tangs were still suspicious of them.

ne day Ori Tang did not return from swing school with the other children. The orangutan children seemed to be nervous and upset, and they chattered amongst themselves. The king sternly asked them what had happened to his baby.

Tessa Tang said he was talking to their bird friend, Holly Hoopoe.

Olivia Tang said he was chasing Brenda Butterfly.

Ginger Tang said he was swinging toward the river with Figgy the Frog hopping after him.

Zoey Tang said he was doing somersaults in the forest.

Toni Tang said he was looking for mangosteens.

Max Tang said he boasted that he was going to look for One-Fang Flossie!

Holly Hoopoe

Figgy
the frog

winging

Mangosteens

Brenda Butterfly

POANI
CODDLES
DEGG
SAFARI
TOURS

Banana peels

OH, DEAR! ONE-FANG FLOSSIE?
Where was ORI TANG??

Finally, Jordan and Jared Tang admitted that Kirstin and the other young orangutans had told Ori to stop boasting. They called him stubborn and a sissy, and they had made him cry. He ran off, sobbing and angry, shouting: **"I'm not a baby anymore, you know!"** They all saw him pick up a banana and climb on a box with four wheels.

The Tang adults were all very angry and worried. They chastised Ori's sister Kirstin for not protecting her little brother. They did not know what to do, so they told Kirstin and her cousins to sit still and not move while they had a conference.

Alone, they chattered and cried and scratched. Somehow, they had to find Ori Tang. Finally, at the advice of the other apes, King Tang took the strongest ape, his brother Uncle Cinnamon, to go out and look for his lost child.

After hours of searching the dense forest and talking to the birds, they found Holly Hoopoe, a handsome black and white bird. King Tang and Uncle Cinnamon made faces at the smelly nest that Holly was guarding. Holly was most insulted and started squawking angrily. She told them that her nest smelled awful so that other birds and animals, including orangutans, wouldn't go near it. No one was going to steal HER eggs. Those eggs were going to become beautiful hoopoe babies. The orangutans apologized and asked if she knew where Ori Tang had gone.

Holly said he ran toward a box on wheels and two very, very ugly creatures gave him some bananas and dragged him away. Holly offered to lead them toward the big river where there was a strange camp.

The two brother orangutans swung on vines toward the river with Holly Hoopoe flying overhead. They crept toward the water. Old Allie Croc was sleeping. Not too far up the hill was an odd sight. The two brothers clambered up the hill and hid in a large tree so they could see what was going on.

The apes had seen the two-legged animals they called "men" before, but this time, these strange creatures had a large box on wheels and a pointed, hollow tent! The tree was quite bare, and King Tang and Uncle Cinnamon kept silent—they didn't want the two strange creatures to see or hear them. There was a man and a woman human, and yes, they were very, very ugly. The woman human held Ori Tang by one of his arms. Ori was wiggling and wriggling and kicking and spitting and yelping, but it didn't do any good. He was then shoved into a small, cramped, but sturdy wooden crate. Brenda Butterfly fluttered about and Figgy the Frog was hopping and croaking furiously, but no one paid any attention to them. Ori Tang howled and sucked his thumb.

The two orangutans sat quietly in the tree. They scratched their heads and pondered. They did not want to be discovered by the very, very ugly humans, so they decided to wait until it was dark. The very, very ugly humans went into their tent and left Ori Tang whimpering outside in the small, cramped, wooden crate. Uncle Cinnamon wanted to grab the crate immediately, but King Tang, being a more sensible ape, thought it best to wait until it was dark. He then asked Holly Hoopoe to find some friends to stir up a racket.

When the moon rose, Holly and her friends were all hidden in the bush, ready to create loud, threatening noises. Suddenly there was a strange, eerie silence. The animals and birds were all paralyzed with fear. They sensed another danger. From the other side of the forest came fierce growling and loud, terrible roars. It was One-Fang Flossie. Uncle Cinnamon thought he saw her tail, but no more. Another loud and terrifying roar followed and then another. The forest creatures realized it was a signal to carry on with their plan.

One-Fang Flossie was helping them!

Apes and monkeys, tapirs, rhinos, snakes, and birds all began to howl and shout, whistle and spit. They hissed and hooted. They hollered and shrieked. They croaked and squealed and snarled. And One-Fang Flossie roared!

The very, very ugly humans ran outside the tent shouting,

"TIGER! HELP! TIGER!!!"

n their terror they tripped, bumped into each other, and rolled down to the edge of the river.

Allie Croc yawned and scared them even further. Seeing the crocodile slither rapidly toward them with her jaws wide open, they stood up and scrambled up the hill, shaking and quaking and screaming in fear. They ran and hid inside their box on wheels. That box on wheels then moved rapidly along the path and out of sight.

King Tang leaped toward the poacher's camp and grabbed the crate with Ori Tang inside. He threw the crate to his brother, Uncle Cinnamon, and the two big apes disappeared deep into the forest. The two brothers swung on vines, tossing the crate from one ape to the other while Holly Hoopoe happily chirped and led the way. Figgy the Frog and Brenda Butterfly followed along too. Ori Tang began to feel "vine-sick." He was really quite dizzy.

**W**hen they got home there was much rejoicing.

Uncle Cinnamon tried to break open the crate with his huge fists.

Bang! Bang! Thud! Thud!

That only gave Ori Tang a headache. He saw twelve Brenda Butterflies and fourteen Figgy the Frogs. He gave a loud belch and started to hiccup. He hiccupped and hiccupped.

Teena, Ori's mom, was furious. She stamped her feet and jumped up and down. She shouted, **"Don't you hurt my baby, you big ape!"**

Ori's hiccups got louder and louder.

King Tang heaved the crate at a large tree. That made matters worse. Ori Tang thought he was going to be sick. He moaned and groaned, and then the poor little orangutan threw up many banana peels.

Teena ran around in circles in a rage, screaming at the two male orangutans. King Tang and Uncle Cinnamon pounded their chests in despair.

The forest came alive with chattering and screeching, bellowing and hollering.

"Save Ori Tang! Set him free!" was their cry.

Teena gathered the female apes together for a conference. "We must use our strong arms in a different way. Our mates are too rough!"

inally, Teena Tang and the female orangutans attached a vine to each side of the crate and they had a tug-of-war. They pulled and they pulled, but the box wouldn't budge. The male apes joined in and they all pulled and pulled. The crate finally fell apart, slats flying in the air.

Ori Tang was FREE!

He felt dizzy and he had a headache, but he was happy to be home with his family. Ori told his cousins that he rode in a moving box with four wheels, but it was more fun to swing on vines.

All the orangutan children apologized to Ori for calling him a sissy and told him they were glad he was safe. They all agreed that he was very brave.

Ori promised his family that he would try not to boast too much, even though he would like to find One-Fang Flossie and thank her for her help. **"After all, I'm not a baby anymore,"** he said.

King Tang looked angry. Teena Tang looked concerned. Uncle Cinnamon looked shocked, and the younger orangutans started to make faces. Then all the orangutans began to talk at once—chattering, scratching, and arguing—as orangutans do. Ori realized he was boasting again. He looked up at his family and he promised solemnly that he would never ever, ever wander off again.

His mother nursed him, gave him a mangosteen, and put him to bed.

HELLO! I'm a FRIENDIMAL™!

My name is Ori Tang, the baby orangutan, and my mother's name is Teena. We are your ENDANGERED ANIMAL FRIENDS! My name, "orangutan," means "man of the woods." Some people call me "orange man" since I resemble a human. I used to live all over Asia, but now I am only found in Indonesia, on the islands of Sumatra and Borneo.

I am a primate—a shy and gentle ape. I am also very strong. I have long arms and a shaggy body, and I love to swing on vines. Like other apes, I have no tail. I swing from vine to vine until I get too old and heavy. Then I sit and eat a lot.

I live with my family in trees deep in the forests. My mother has one baby at a time. It takes about eight and a half months, and we live to be about forty years old. I eat mostly plants, but I like eggs and shellfish, too! My favorite foods are mangosteens, bananas, and durians—all smelly, delicious fruits!

My natural enemies are tigers, and some snakes.

My unnatural enemies are loggers, the threat of diminishing forests, kidnappers, and the threat of being sold as a pet on the black market.

YOU CAN HELP PROTECT ME FROM MY ENEMIES!
PROTECT ME!   PAMPER ME!   PLAY WITH ME!

Do Animals Cry?

Do animals LOVE like me, like you?
 Do animals know to love?
Do animals love—indeed they do
 Yes, animals feel and love!

They protect their babies and feed their young
 They teach them how to grow big and strong
They nestle and wrestle, they kiss and they coo
 They snuggle and cuddle, they purr and they mieuw
Yes—animals LOVE!

Yes, animals CRY when they're not free and
 Animals TALK like you, like me
And animals SING and they SMILE and they PLAY
 Yes—animals LOVE!

Thank You

To all you wonderful humans at Brown Books, a very special thank you.
Milli Brown, Kathryn Grant, Ted Ruybal, Cindy Birne . . . you're the greatest.
You and your staff helped bring us to life.

Love and orang hugs,

ORI TANG

and the orangutans

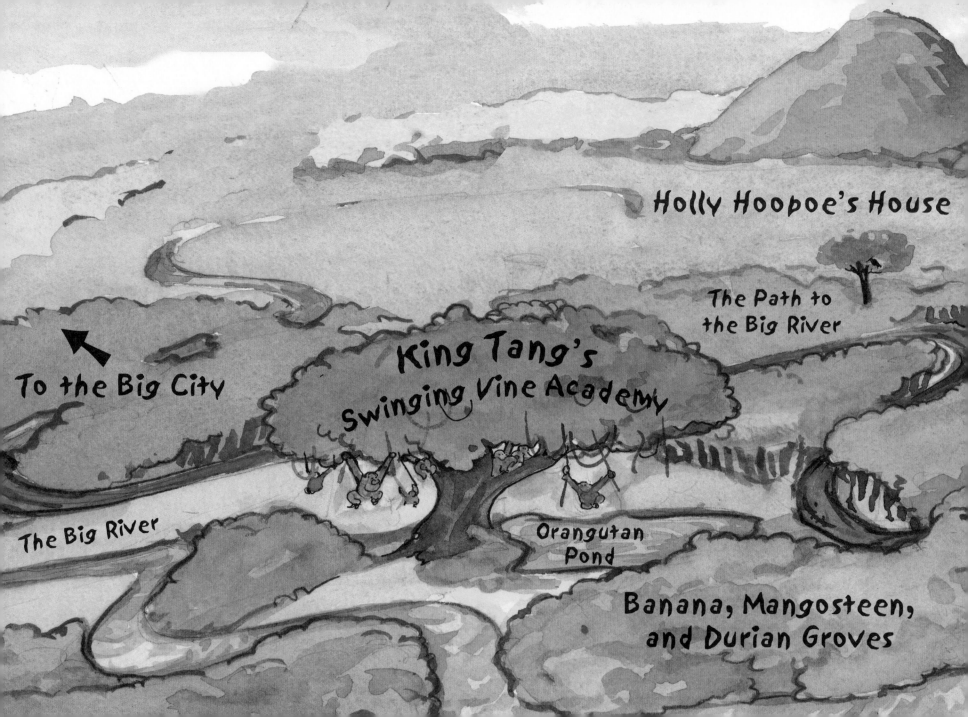